BODYGUARD'S BBW LITTLE

Age Play DDlg Small Town Romance

Amanda King

Copyright © 2022 Amanda King

All rights reserved

The characters and events portrayed in this book are fictitious. Any similarity to real persons, living or dead, is coincidental and not intended by the author.

No part of this book may be reproduced, or stored in a retrieval system, or transmitted in any form or by any means, electronic, mechanical, photocopying, recording, or otherwise, without express written permission of the publisher.

ISBN: 9798352896976
Imprint: Independently published

1st edition

CONTENTS

CHAPTER 1

Myrna

I knew he was a Daddy and it was no secret. Nothing about it could be after we all began to find out about the secret lifestyle that was spreading in all parts of the city.

I was in the stands and watching him from afar. It was a basketball game. It wasn't a professional game, and it really couldn't be. They were just playing together. Even the stadium where we were was pretty small and only for some people to be watching the game.

Being in the stands, I was pretty much alone. I had my friend, who I texted sometimes, but tonight she was unavailable. I didn't even know what happened. One moment we were texting without any issue and then her boyfriend sent me a message demanding that I stopped chatting with her.

His reasons? They were pretty obvious, even though I couldn't make sense of them when they were first brought up. He said that my texting her so often was creating a rift in their relationship. I didn't even know that that was happening.

Everything was just so convoluted that, in the end, I felt bad about it even though my friend told me so many times I didn't have to worry about anything.

I took a deep breath. My eyes were only focused on the basketball player running with the ball toward his objective. There was something different about his body. I didn't want to come off as a creep, but he was just so dreamy.

His muscles were nothing short of perfect. He had just enough body fat in his body to better highlight his curves without looking like a gym freak. I wondered how I would feel if, one day, I were allowed to run my fingers over his curves. I didn't think it would ever happen, but I could always dream.

So many times, just before going to sleep, I always masturbated. Every time that happened, I thought about Marc. I thought about him mounting me and fucking me until I cried out his name over and over. I dreamed about him taking my virginity, something I was sure would never happen.

I sighed again, pulling down the hood of my jacket. I didn't want anyone in the stands to recognize me. I was an influencer. I influenced people and, more often than not, I also ran campaigns asking my followers to take certain actions.

My main channel was on TikTok. Even though I didn't make a lot of money, it was enough to pay my rent and I even managed to save some money, which was more than enough to keep me afloat.

I just couldn't stop scrutinizing every part of his body. His muscles seemed to move with such grace, sweat drops dribbling down his skin, his eyes focused only on what was ahead. He maneuvered through the other team's members without difficulty and then he jumped, sinking the ball into the net with ease. Even the other team's members around him fell away from him as though he was a force of nature.

I was impressed. I never thought that I would see someone, who was nothing more than an amateur basketball player, with such a natural ability to score.

I stood up moments later when it was clear that the basketball match was already reaching its end. My eyes were still glued to Marc, though. He was wiping his forehead with a handkerchief. My eyes couldn't stop examining the way that his muscles shifted and bulged. The sweat dribbling down his skin was the cherry on top.

Certain that nothing tonight was going to happen and that I

needed to catch some sleep, I began to make my way toward the exit of the stadium. Calling it a stadium was actually overstating its dimensions, but I didn't really give a damn about that.

But just when I was almost exiting the stadium, I felt as though someone was looking at me. Call it a sixth sense or something like that, but I just really felt as though someone was watching me from afar.

I froze up where I was and turned around slowly. I didn't want to spook whoever was studying me so closely.

I thought I was going to find someone who recognized me as the influencer I was, but then I realized that the person that was having such an effect on me was actually none other than Marc himself. He was still holding the handkerchief in his hands.

He knew I was a Little, so what was he thinking? He was famous here in this town. People would begin to talk about it if he got caught eyeing a woman like me from a distance like this. They would all begin to talk about it and his girlfriend, who was living across the country, would hear everything and they would break up. Great. Another break-up because of me. I could already imagine that happening and I wouldn't be able to do anything to stop it. Another sleepless night thinking about it.

But then, he returned his attention to his friends who were approaching him. They began to talk about something, which relieved me. I thought that they were going to talk about me, especially after figuring out that influencer Myrna was watching him from afar.

But that wasn't what was happening, so I had enough time to go back to my home. And I did that some minutes later while walking with my head lowered and my hood covering part of it. Upon getting there, I closed the door with my key and then fell onto the bed, nestling Mr. Coco in my arms and clutching him to me strongly. I began to whimper. Even though I liked to think I was doing well in life, it was sometimes difficult to keep that in mind when I was so lonely and I didn't have much hope I would ever find a boyfriend that would also be my Daddy.

It just couldn't happen. Even though more Daddies were

beginning to show up here in town, they were always taken. Maybe I was meant to be alone for the rest of my life.

CHAPTER 2

Harold

Tic tac, tic tac so the clock went over and over as the seconds continued to pass. I was in my house and holding a portrait with me and my girlfriend in it.

Things were so better between us years ago, but now they had already begun to lose intensity. I didn't do anything wrong, so I couldn't be part of the problem.

I took another sip of the beer I was holding in my hand. It was cheap, but I didn't really care. As long as the alcohol was good enough for me, then it was also good enough to push away the evil thoughts in my mind.

I kept wondering if Michelle wasn't seeing someone else behind my back. It wouldn't be the first time if that was the case. It hurt me to be thinking about it. The first time that I learned she was cheating on me, I thought we were going to break up, but in the end, I didn't choose to do that, imagining that we could still salvage our relationship.

We had sex so many times after that, but it wasn't like it was before. I didn't think it would ever be, to be honest.

Another sip from the beer bottle I was holding in my hand. The TV was showing a series I didn't really care about. As long as I had some background noise, then for me, it was great.

I took a deep breath, thinking about someone else. I wasn't

going to cheat on Michelle no matter what happened. Maybe I should be entitled to someone else, but it wasn't going to happen.

Not as long as I didn't have solid proof she was seeing someone else.

I stood up and I made my way to the window. This was a small city and I felt so lonely right now. I was a bodyguard, but I was looking for a job. For the time being, the only thing I had to pass the time was my amateur career in basketball.

It wasn't really going to take me anywhere, though. I only made some money thanks to the reels I uploaded on Instagram. I sold some merchandise that way, so for the time being, it was enough to pay the rent and some other necessities that came with living here.

At least, living in such a small city and far from everything meant that I didn't have to spend a lot of money on anything of the sort.

Why was I holding this beer bottle in my hand and why was I drinking so much even though it wasn't going to actually make me feel better? I asked myself, kicking myself for falling into the same addiction over and over, and thinking that it was going to take me anywhere.

It wasn't, though.

I took a deep breath and then I put the bottle down on the table by my side. What should I do right now? I should take a shower and then check if I had something in my email account.

If there was anything, I was going to be notified and that was going to be it. Then, I would check up with whoever had sent me the email and we would talk about the payment and maybe I would finally have more money than I had right now. After all, I had to think about my future, and right now that could be saving up some money so that I could invest it.

I took a shower, put on my pajamas, and then I sat behind my computer. I turned it on and then I began to check what the screen was showing, and more specifically what was in my inbox and if there was anything new that caught my attention.

So far, there didn't appear to be anything out of the ordinary other than some spam emails which wouldn't actually help me with anything. They were just a waste of time.

I took a deep breath in, put my hands behind my head, stretched my back, and then when I was finally going to give up for the night and focus on something else, my eyes noticed something on the screen.

It was an email from someone that wasn't a company or that was clearly only trying to steal my password.

The title of the email was: *Please, I need your help.*

I clicked on the email in a heartbeat and began to read what was in the body part of it.

I don't know who else to ask for help right now. I think someone's trying to kill me. I'm an influencer, so it wouldn't be the first time it's happening. I want to make sure I'm not going to die the next time that I walk out of my apartment. Can you help me? You are the only one in town that does this. You are the only bodyguard I know about, so I think you are the only one I can ask for help right now.

And then, there was also her name at the bottom of the email.

Myrna Latham.

She was a Little, no denying it. Now that, in town, everyone was coming out after realizing that feeling so much paranoia about everyone's acceptance of it, all the Littles and Daddies were coming out and making their lifestyle known.

It was great.

I never thought that I would, one day, be paired with Myrna Latham. She was an influencer and she was pretty vocal about our community. She had her opinions and she was always controversial, so if someone was trying to kill her, it wouldn't be too surprising, but I also didn't want to find myself stuck with her.

In her same apartment, sharing everything. To be her bodyguard... I just never thought that the day would come.

But she was kinda rich and she had enough money to pay for my services, so I still had to do this.

Michelle would most likely never even find out anything about it.

She didn't even call me anymore, after all.

CHAPTER 3

Myrna

I had gotten back from the stadium when my eyes noticed a small piece of paper lying on the floor in front of the door to my apartment. I had picked it up and then read what was written on it. It was at that moment that I gasped, thinking that my life was over.

If you are really thinking you are going to get away with everything you've done, then think again. I'm coming for you. You should take back everything you've said in that latest video you've made.

You should never antagonize the church. We are so much more important than everyone else in town. We are going to make sure that you regret everything you've said about our father. He is the most respected man in the world.

Take it all back and maybe we can come to an agreement where we would only beat you up slowly and nicely. Maybe we would even knock out some teeth. Nothing really out of the ordinary. I'm certain that you are someone with a good heart and we can begin to talk about this more carefully once you've finished your part.

As always, I'm an avid enjoyer of your videos, so I'm going to be waiting for your video to be uploaded in the next couple of hours. You only have a few. I'm not someone that exercises a lot of patience, so I want you to keep that in mind.

After reading that, I had dropped the piece of paper back on the ground and then I ran inside my apartment and I had even locked the door with the key. Nobody could come in and nobody would.

I should tell the police about this was the first thing that crossed my mind and I did that, but I felt it wasn't going to be sufficient. Victor told me that the department was stretched thin and he couldn't order any of his deputies to keep watch over the building where I lived. Even though I couldn't read what he was thinking, I was pretty certain he thought that there was nothing substantial about the threat.

Or maybe he just didn't like me much, given the way that I also antagonized the sheriff's department, too. Well, I always made sure not to spare anyone, and the department was no exception.

His not helping me was why I did this. It was why I begged for Harold's help.

He had already called and told me he was going to come tonight. Remembering that he was a Daddy, I couldn't stop feeling slightly fearful about what might happen if he started to live with me.

He would have to, right? I asked myself. Of course that he was going to do that. Otherwise, he wouldn't be a bodyguard, and paying for his services would be pointless. At least, that was how I looked at it.

I heard his pickup truck pulling over in front of the apartment. It had to be him. I even looked out the window and found him coming over. I had already told the receptionist on the ground floor that he could come up to my apartment, and thus he should have no problems with that. Not to mention that I didn't feel like getting out of my bedroom for no reason at all, so he should come up and find me curled up in my bedsheets.

The only problem with that, though, was the fact that my entire apartment was such a mess right now. Everything was out of place, all my toys scattered all over, the smell coming from the kitchen – I had just finished cooking dinner - and my bathroom was also wet after I took my shower.

He was going to notice all that and then he would tell everyone in town I couldn't take care of myself. Word would spread around and I would become the joke around here. Just thinking about that happening, I already felt ripples of fear snaking in me. It only made me feel even more paranoid about what was going to happen.

That was why I was clutching Mr. Coco to me as much as I could. He was coconut-brown and so cute, even though he was also slightly weathered and was also looking old. Not much I could do about that, though. I wouldn't buy another like him and even if I did, it wouldn't be what I was looking for. When it came to Mr. Coco, he was the only one that existed for me.

Knocks came from the door. It had to be Harold, so I was already bracing myself for what living with him was going to mean. If it wasn't for the threat, this wouldn't be happening. I had such a huge crush on him and now we were going to be spending time under the same roof.

Part of me should be happy and indeed it was, but the other part of me was terrified. More so than it was with the threat.

"Myrna?" He knocked on the door again. "It's me, Harold. I've come here to talk a little bit more about our arrangement. I want you to show me what you've said before about the threat."

Getting out of bed was almost impossible, but I still did it. Dragging myself over to the door was even more difficult, but again I still did it. In no time at all, I found myself behind the door, and then I opened it slowly and didn't move it all the way. There was only a tiny gap that let me see Harold and it was good enough.

His eyes examined me slowly and carefully. What was he thinking? I asked myself.

Then, he cleared his throat. "Are you going to let me inside or not? I don't want to be rude, but you've told me that you are fearing for your life, so I want to make sure that nothing weird is happening here."

CHAPTER 4

Harold

Myrna was standing behind the door and, so far, she still didn't open it. Time passed and this was becoming more uncomfortable than I'd thought.

"Hmmm, Myrna?" I asked, hoping that she was going to snap back to reality.

"Yeah, it's me. I'm here. I'm going to open the door for you in a bit," she said and then I stepped inside the apartment. Wow. It looked like a mess. She didn't take care of herself at all or her apartment, for that matter.

Well, to be honest, more often than not Littles like her didn't, so this wasn't too surprising. I just wished that I could do something about it. Still, I wasn't going to bring that up. Doing that wouldn't help me with anything, and I didn't want to spook her more than she already was.

"It's that piece of paper behind you," she said, pointing at it. I went on one knee and picked it up. It said everything she'd mentioned before. Myrna certainly didn't lie. It could be that the threat comes from a prank, though. As for the search behind it, that was up to the sheriff's department. I didn't have to do anything about it right now. For the time being, my job was to keep Myrna protected.

"Yeah, I see. So, someone is really out to get you. Don't worry.

As long as I'm around, nothing will happen."

Looking around the living room – which was adjacent to the kitchen in the apartment – I was kind of surprised. I thought that I was going to come into the apartment of someone a little messy, but I didn't think it was going to be so bad.

I wasn't going to say anything about that, though.

"Thank you. Do you want something to eat?" She asked. How nice. Her voice was really sweet, especially when she wasn't yapping about anything on her videos. I watched them from time to time.

Maybe it was a hidden desire in me that wanted to make me have something with her, but again, nothing would ever happen between us because I was with Michelle.

Not to mention that I didn't want all the drama that would come with being with Myrna.

"Well, do you want anything? I think that I'm going to be in my bedroom. I already feel so much safer now that you are here with me."

"It's okay. I'm going to be here in the living room and watching for anything suspicious. For the time being, Victor is going to keep one of the cruisers parked in front of the building. If anyone tries anything, they will most likely be caught and arrested. The good thing is that, thanks to your work, you don't really have to go out often, so you are as safe as you can be."

"Other than buying groceries, that is."

"I can do that for you or we can arrange for someone to fill in that role."

"Maybe we should do the latter. I don't want to be alone now that I know someone is out to get me."

"Talking about that, that person mentioned something about a church. Are they talking about the church in town?"

"I don't really know. I hope that you can tell me something about that."

"I'm not a detective. I wish I could go out and poke around a little with the information we have, but I don't think that's part of my job."

She wrung her hands together, her hair looking a little messy right now. Again, with my Daddy side coming out, the only thing I wanted to do was to fix it and then maybe give her a haircut, but that would make my stay here weird, and thus it was a no-no to me.

Given the way that Myrna was behaving, she was already kind of feeling that way, anyway.

"Of course, of course. You don't have to do anything other than what we agreed on."

"I'm happy you understand that."

There was a moment of silence while I thought about what to say next. I turned around slowly in the living room, finding myself bothered by all the mess. Couldn't I make at least one exception to what I said before?

Maybe I could and maybe I should.

I rubbed the back of my head with my hand. "I don't know how to say this, but it's kind of dirty in here. Don't you want me to do something about that?"

She gasped, her cheeks blushing. "Uh-oh, I don't know. It's just like you said. I don't want you to do anything other than what was agreed on in the contract. You are here to protect me and do nothing more than that, even though I would like that you did a couple of other things for me…"

She chuckled, blushing harder. The way that she was wringing her hands together, it was obvious that she didn't intend to do that. Myrna never intended to say the words that came out of her mouth. It just slipped out.

I ignored her words. No point in making Myrna feel more uncomfortable than she was already.

"Well, it doesn't really matter to me. If I'm going to be living here with you together, then I want to make this space a little more livable."

"Oh. That's okay. I don't really have time to clean it up, but if you want to do that, then it's okay."

There was another awkward moment of silence. I kept on wondering what she was thinking and why she found it so difficult to find a Daddy in the city. After all, it wasn't like there wasn't anyone around available. There were some candidates and they had to be good enough for her.

"Well, I'm going to my bedroom right now and hopefully I can get some sleep. It's going to be difficult, thinking about the death threat all the time."

"Don't worry. I'm going to be here in the living room and I'm going to be watching over anything that happens in here and outside."

"Thanks."

And after saying that, Myrna whirled around and disappeared inside her bedroom, locking the door behind her.

She was fast doing that. It was almost like she didn't want to spend another minute with me. I couldn't imagine that she was going to come out and see me often in the living room.

Most likely, she was going to be avoiding me as much as she could from this moment onwards.

CHAPTER 5

Myrna

He said he didn't want to be living in my apartment because of all the mess I left. To be honest, under other circumstances and when I wasn't so worried about the death threats, that was exactly what I would've done. I would have cleaned it up thoroughly and left the place looking tidy and neat.

I was so ashamed when he said those words to me. He was a Daddy, so that was certainly just that side of him speaking louder than any other. He wanted to fix me and make me feel less uncomfortable with myself, but that was difficult. If there was something that I learned about myself growing up, it was that it was difficult for me to let other people into my life.

Harold was my crush, but that would never change.

I was still inside my bedroom and now was a couple of hours since he arrived. I wondered what was going on in his mind. The walls of the place were pretty thin, so I knew that Harold had to be cleaning up the apartment, considering the level of noise that he was making.

He wasn't even going to charge me anything more for that, I thought with a smile on my face.

To be honest, only one person could make me feel comfortable right now, and that was Mr. Coco. He was lying on the mattress by my side and gazing at me with concerned yet captivating eyes.

If he was ever capable of speaking, I could already imagine what he would be saying to me.

The fact that he's so worried about you means that he cares about you. More so than you think.

"I don't think that he actually cares about me. Not in that sense, anyway."

Talking to Mr. Coco wasn't weird to me. I used to do it all the time now.

You don't even know that. You are only lying to yourself.

I couldn't deny that I felt something strong for Harold, but that was all it was. I would never suddenly find myself making such a big mistake in my life.

Even though it was making me lower my hand as I looked for my pussy, it would never break me out of my shell.

At least, that was what I was telling myself as I began to rub my pussy with my fingers slowly and carefully. Being a virgin, I wanted to be fucked for the first time in my life, and even though I had one of the hottest men of all time in my apartment, nothing was going to happen.

My body was beginning to heat up as I thought about Harold without his clothes. I could just imagine him with his muscles flexing and bulging. His girlfriend was so lucky, not gonna lie.

But there was no point in continuing this and fomenting the thought that just sprouted up in my mind. Even though rubbing my finger on my clit was exciting and was creating waves of pleasure in my body, I knew that I shouldn't fool myself with my dreams.

Not to mention that it was the dead of the night and I had to get out of bed after realizing that I didn't fill my water bottle. It was sitting there on top of the computer desk, and my throat was dry right now.

I sighed, slipping out from under the blanket, and then I padded over to the door. I opened it slowly and carefully after thinking that, since it was some hours after his arrival, he had to be sleeping on the couch. I didn't think about that at all. I didn't even try to find a solution so that he could sleep somewhere better.

I walked out into the hallway and I found him still awake. Of course that Harold was going to be awake. He came here to protect me and that was the only reason why he was going to be paid. It was going to take a huge hit to my bank account, but it was better this way than to be fearing for my life all the time.

With Harold around, I was already feeling much safer.

He wasn't lying on the couch as I'd thought. He was sitting at the table in the kitchen, his hand holding his pistol. He looked absolutely confident handling it. He was cleaning it with a handkerchief, looking at me when he realized that I was coming.

I opened my mouth, but he was the one that spoke first. "Nothing unusual has happened so far, Mrs. Latham. Everything is okay here."

"You don't really need to call me that. I'm a Little, remember? I find it weird whenever someone refers to me as though I'm older than they are."

He smiled. "Duly noted. I'm not going to call you 'Mrs. Latham' again." He took a deep breath, his eyes scanning the environment. "I cleaned up the apartment. It looks better now. Do you want me to do the same to your bedroom?"

I waved my hand, proceeding to the sink. Even though it wasn't recommended to drink water from the tap, I didn't have enough money to buy bottled water. I could, but then I would have to forgo buying some of the candies I most loved, and that wasn't something I was okay with.

CHAPTER 6

Harold

She looked so pretty. Her shirt was almost plain white if it wasn't for the drawing of a Disney cartoon on it. The Little Mermaid. Red hair, freckles on her cheeks, snow-white skin, and a long green tail. It was pretty and unlike some of the things I had noticed in her apartment, the shirt wasn't old and weathered. It was almost brand new. I took that as a sign that Myrna didn't save money when it came to spending on her lifestyle.

Good. She really shouldn't do that. I would buy her something to bring a smile back to her face if I wasn't so short on cash right now, to be honest.

So, was Myrna going to reply to my question? I sure as hell hoped so. I wasn't accustomed to being left in the void after making a question.

"Sure. Why not?"

I blinked twice in a row. I didn't think Myrna was going to be so straight with her answer. I thought that Myrna was going to hide behind it.

My eyes scanned her from top to bottom. She was so delicate, making my dick give some somersaults under my pants. I shifted my legs so that she couldn't see my boner. Thankfully, she couldn't even if she was trying.

Myrna proceeded to the sink, filled her bottle with water, and when she was going back to her bedroom, she stopped.

She turned to look at me and I noticed a funny smile spreading on her face.

"Right, you said you were going to clean up my bedroom."

How uncomfortable she was looking right now. I wanted so much to wrap her in my arms and tell her that everything was okay. She was almost making a big mess out of something so simple.

I was only going to be cleaning up her bedroom, nothing more than that. Of course, that meant seeing some of the things she was keeping hidden from me.

Maybe she thought that I was going to stumble on her dildo or something of the sort? But even if that happened, I wouldn't even blink at it. Did she think she was the only one with a dildo here in this town?

I went to her bedroom after saying, "it's not going to take long. Even though it's late at night, you are going to appreciate sleeping in a cleaner place."

"Right, of course," she said under her breath. I took everything to her bedroom and examined the place with my eyes. Nothing about it stood odd to me. Nothing should, given that this wasn't the first time that I was visiting a Little's bedroom. I thought that I was going to immediately find her dildo, but even if she had it, it wasn't out in the open, as it shouldn't be.

I started to clean up her bedroom while being aware that she was right behind me, biting her fingernails. Myrna was so concerned that I was going to find something almost incriminating in her bedroom, but even if there was, it couldn't be anything terrifying.

A couple of minutes later, which couldn't have been more than half an hour, the place was tidy and everything was clean. I turned in an instant and found Myrna still standing behind me. She wore a pair of tiny shorts, which highlighted the curves of her legs.

"Thank you. It really looks so much better right now," she confessed and didn't even give me any time to say anything else before she rushed inside her bedroom. In a moment, she was throwing herself onto the bed and taking her stuffed toy in her hands. He was from a cartoon that I remembered quite well. Michelle watched it sometimes, though not as often as in the past anymore. It kind of made me wonder if she wasn't walking away from being a Little...

I was worried about Myrna's well-being now more than anything else. Should I do it? Should I offer my support? Doing so tempted me, but then again, I didn't want to do anything that might be weird.

I did hear a whimper coming from inside her room when she locked the door. She was avoiding me so much she didn't even say more than that thank you.

I just couldn't let things end like this, so I was obviously going to do something I would regret later.

I knocked on the door. For a moment, Myrna didn't say anything. When I knocked again, she barked, "what do you want? It's not even your first night in my apartment, and you are already kind of annoying me."

"I just want to make sure that you are okay. I thought that I heard you crying."

"I'm not crying. I don't know what you're talking about."

"Well, maybe you should be a little bit more forthcoming with me. After all, I'm a Daddy and, if you need anything, I'm here for you."

"What does it matter that you are a Daddy when nothing can ever happen between us?"

She was right about that. Even though Myrna was single, even if I weren't with Michelle, nothing could happen between us. She was an influencer and I was the kind of person that didn't want any spotlight on me.

"I'm just saying that if you need someone to talk about anything, I'm here."

There was a moment of silence. Myrna didn't say anything, but then she changed her attitude in the blink of an eye.

She opened the door and wasn't crying, even though I could see she was doing everything in her power to hide the tears.

"See? I'm not crying. You don't need to worry so much about me. I'm an adult. I can take care of myself."

That wasn't exactly true, and if she was so certain that this was going to end right now, then she was going to be disappointed.

Sometimes, obsessions like this one emerged in my mind and I couldn't get rid of them.

CHAPTER 7

Myrna

"So, how come someone like you is still single?" He asked me, holding the glass of juice in his hand. He took sips from it every so often when his throat was dry.

I shifted on the couch. We were watching TV. It was a late-night cartoon that played sometimes. Late-night cartoons weren't a common thing anymore, with most children watching snippets of old shows on their phones. I suspected that it was going to remain like that for quite some time, which was sad.

Despite our initial confrontation about Harold's boundaries with me, we were beginning to bond and get to know each other better. This was one such moment.

Of course, he was sitting all the way on the other side of the couch. Chances were he just wanted to avoid me worrying he wanted to take advantage of me. I knew he never would, so he didn't need to worry about that.

As usual, I was with Mr. Coco. More often than not, I found that he was the only one that could truly understand me.

"I don't know. I guess that I've never been open to relationships."

He snorted. "C'mon, that can't be true. You have to be hiding something from me."

I wasn't hiding anything from Harold. I just didn't think that anything would ever happen between me and a guy. Again, I spent most of my time locked up in my bedroom and it probably wouldn't change in the next few years.

"I'm not hiding anything from you, smart ass," I joked before throwing the pillow at him. It hit his shoulder as he smiled. His teeth shone brightly under the light bulb hanging from the ceiling.

"Careful. I might decide to punish you if you keep that up. I don't like it when Littles like you throw stuff at me."

"Does Michelle do the same?"

Harold blinked twice. "Michelle? What about her?"

"I asked you if she also throws stuff at you."

He looked away, staring out the window. Was it just me or did he look pensive right now?

Harold wore different clothes tonight. They hung tightly on his body, showing off his curves. They were round and I knew that his muscles were stiff but also soft to the touch. After all, there had been this moment when I bumped into him when he was stepping out of the bathroom, and I felt that then.

We shared the same bathroom, so every time that I went to the shower after he did, I felt his smell and that was always one of the best things about my days.

Harold shook his head when he realized I was still waiting for his answer.

"Don't worry about Michelle. She does throw stuff at me sometimes, though, answering your question."

An awkward moment of pause settled between us. I wondered if I should push on the little topic that sprouted up between us.

Maybe I should. Since I was going to be living with Harold for who knew how much longer and he even cooked for me - something I never thought would happen between us – we should get to know each other better.

"That was a little worrying. Is there something happening between you two that you want to tell me about?"

In the meantime, my eyes couldn't stop glancing down and finding his bulge. He didn't have an erection, but he might as well be having it. His bulge was just so big and plump. I could imagine myself, again, with my hands all over it and then sneaking them under his pants…

It would never happen, though. He was still with Michelle and, if there was something I learned growing up, it was that I could never try to separate a man from his loved one.

"I don't think there's anything I want to tell you about. Plus, for a Little like you, I think that you should already be sleeping, don't you agree?"

"But I don't want to sleep right now, Daddy." We were role-playing after agreeing that we could do this without him feeling that he was cheating on Michelle. The more I thought about it, the more I realized that Harold was pretty open-minded. Michelle was so lucky to be with him. "I want to watch more of the Little Mermaid movie, actually."

"C'mon, it's pretty late tonight already and you haven't even told me why you've never had a boyfriend. It's so puzzling. You are pretty and sexy, you know that, right?"

He shot that question at me as though it was the most normal thing in the world to say. I almost jumped where I was sitting on the couch.

It was surprising, but not at all unexpected. Harold was only reiterating the question he'd made earlier, after all.

I mumbled and couldn't quite come up with the right words. The only good thing about this moment right now was that I still had Mr. Coco in my hands. He was, just like so many other times, the only one comforting me right now.

I supposed I couldn't keep running away from that question. When it came to being persistent about anything, Harold didn't stop obsessing about it until he got what he needed.

"It's so difficult for me to talk about it."

"Why's that?" He asked, shifting closer to me.

"The truth is that I just always find it so difficult to let anyone further in my life other than sharing a couple of things with them."

There. I said it. I never thought I would be talking about

something so personal to me, but it happened and I couldn't do anything about that anymore.

He shifted a little closer to me as though he knew I was begging to feel the warmth of his body.

Harold wasn't even that near me yet and I could already feel it. That was how much heat was radiating from his body. I couldn't help bask myself in it for the couple of minutes that this was happening without blacking out all of a sudden.

"That's a shame, really. You shouldn't shield yourself from people as much as you keep doing."

CHAPTER 8

Myrna

But that was so difficult to do. "Every time I let someone in my life, it ends up hurting me." Harold's arm was on the backrest of the couch. He shouldn't be this near me, and yet he still was.

What was he thinking he was doing? He still had Michelle, so it wasn't like he would dump her for me.

At least, I wasn't betting on that.

"You shouldn't be like that. Sometimes, you do have to let some people in your life."

I sniffled. "It's so difficult for me. You have no idea how many times I came back running to my apartment crying because someone hurt me."

"Well, if it's any consolation, in case that ever happens again from now on, you can tell me everything. I know that you don't have anyone else here in Sudbury, but I would still protect you."

"That's very kind, but I just don't want Michelle to be jealous because of me."

He turned his face to look at the TV screen.

"About Michelle..." He murmured, his eyes glazing over. He was deeply thinking about something. I wondered if it had anything to do with Michelle.

"What about her? Every time that I bring her up, you start to drift away."

"The truth is that things haven't been stellar between us."

"Why is that?" My heart jumped in my chest. By now, I felt like there might be a chance for Harold and me, but I still didn't want to fool myself.

"She isn't in love with me anymore."

My heart gave somersault. Could it really be? Could there really be something that could happen between us?

"What happened? I don't want to feel like I'm prying, but I'm here for you in case you feel like you also don't have anyone you can talk to."

He stood up, keeping his back turned to me. I felt as though he just didn't want to show me his face at the moment.

"I caught her cheating on me with another guy once."

My eyes bulged out in an instant. I knew that Michelle could be wild and didn't usually think about the consequences of her actions, more often than not thinking about herself only, but I never pegged her as a cheater.

"I'm so sorry. I didn't know anything about that. I thought that Michelle loved you. Even though we don't know each other much, you do seem to be such a nice guy. After all, you cleaned up my apartment and didn't even charge more for that. I love your food, too."

He turned around, smiling. Harold wasn't crying to the point of shedding tears, but his eyes were still reddish. I wished I could hug him and tell him that everything was going to be fine. Sometimes, even Daddies needed support from their Littles. The Daddy/Little Girl relationship wasn't a one-way arrangement.

He waved his hand. "It's okay. It doesn't really matter. She's traveling abroad right now and hasn't even been answering my calls. I think that when she comes back, she will probably tell me that she won't want anything with me."

And then this hottie, loving Daddy will be available.

Again, it wasn't like he even felt for me the same things I felt for him, so I still didn't want to fool myself right now with dreams that couldn't come true.

I clutched Mr. Coco more tightly to my chest.

A second later, Harold sat back down on the couch by my side. "I wish I could do something about that."

We were so close to kissing right now. He put his arm back over the backrest of the couch and his eyes were examining me closely. For now, it was like there was a moment of silence starting between us and I had no idea what to do about it. Silence could be too unnerving and stressful sometimes.

"Maybe you could do something about that. Maybe..." He murmured before connecting his lips to mine. It happened slowly and I welcomed it. I could have stopped it. I could have pushed my hand on his chest and he would have moved away from me, but this was my first time kissing and I had been getting to know him so well these last couple of weeks. It felt right to be doing this.

His mannerisms, his favorite food, his OCDs, and pretty much everything about him. I connected with all of them. This couldn't be any different. I thought that we were becoming just friends, but this passionate kiss he was sharing with me was showing me otherwise.

It was wet.

It was hot.

It was everything I needed right now, and I even let out a whimper through my mouth. I felt his lips pressing on my bottom lip, his eyes opening and connecting with me.

Harold didn't move his head away from me when he said, "I've been thinking about this ever since I really started to learn everything I could about you."

"I want this to continue."

"I think the same way. Don't worry about my girlfriend. I don't really think that we are in love anymore, so I'm not cheating on her."

"I'm not worried about her. I'm worried about you. I think that you deserve a Little Girl that actually cares about you."

He sighed, grabbing my hand. His hand was much bigger than mine and it engulfed it, making it feel like nothing, too. It was rough and calloused, which only added to the love I felt for him.

After learning so much about Harold and connecting so well

with him, there was no other word that felt more right to this moment that was materializing between us.

It was love, no denying it.

CHAPTER 9

Harold

It was just a kiss. Nothing more than that, but it did open a new path that I could follow from this moment onwards. Myrna was sleeping in her bed after I pulled her under the blanket.

She was such a sweet Little that I wanted to do something crazy. How about buying her a crib? I could do that. I knew someone who would offer one to me without charging much, so that was what I was relying on.

I smiled, making what was one of the best decisions of my life recently. I dialed his number and then he picked up the call. My buddy asked me what I wanted, and I told him everything.

In the next couple of days, Myrna would wake up with a big change in her life. We would have to find some space for the crib in her place, but it wouldn't be anything different from what she was already used to. Given the size of our place, she always had to find space for what she wanted.

She yawned, stretching her arms out. She noticed that I was in the doorway. I had just gotten here, so I wasn't being a creep by watching her while she slept. I would never do something like that.

Myrna made grabby hands as she said, "hold me, Daddy. Take me up in your arms."

I did that as I swept her up. She threw her arms and legs

around me, pushing herself against my body as much as she could. She was big, but she was still light – at least for me, she was. I felt her pussy pressing against my crotch through my underwear and I loved that.

My dick growing under my pants, the only thing I wanted to do right now was to rip the clothes off her body and finally take our relationship to the next level. Her eyes were locked with mine and I knew that the same thoughts were passing in her mind right now.

"Do you want something to eat? Do you want Daddy to make you your favorite food?"

"Yes, Daddy! That's exactly what I want!" She exclaimed, begging me to make her favorite meal. This morning, her belly was going to be full with my breakfast. She was going to love it. Yogurt, cereal with milk, a fruit smoothie, and pretty much everything else she could want.

I learned that Myrna didn't make as much money as I thought, but it was still more than enough to fill the fridge and the cupboards with everything she wanted.

I went over to the kitchen, started to prepare everything, and before long, it was all ready. Bitty, which was her nickname, clutched Mr. Coco strongly to her chest. She was smiling so happily right now I just wanted to be kissing her cheeks for as long as possible until she begged me to stop.

Before long, I reached her and started to fill her belly with the breakfast I made. She loved everything she was devouring. I could see it in her sunny smile.

When she was finished, she threw her arms around me.

"Come on, I haven't even cleaned all of this in the sink yet. I think I should do that right now, don't you agree?" I asked, hoping that she would understand what was going on in my mind right now.

After stuffing her belly with breakfast, it was time to move to do something that actually stirred my heart.

She was in the mood for it and I could remember that she almost told me she was a virgin. Not to mention that I wanted to be giving her a bath too right now, or brush her teeth, which would be nice as well. It would be only fitting so that we made our relationship more official.

I cleaned the dishes and tidied up the kitchen, and then came back to her with a winning smile on my face - and also a huge boner in my pants.

I approached my hand to Mr. Coco and she moved it away from me and to her chest instantly. I didn't think that she was going to feel threatened.

"There's a surprise that I want to do with you right now and Mr. Coco can't be with us," I pointed out.

She lied down on the couch before she lifted her legs and started to move them as though she was riding a bicycle. Then, she picked up her pacifier and popped it into her mouth.

I put my hands on my waist. She was going to make this difficult for me, wasn't she? I asked myself, smiling that this was happening to me again. I was role-playing with another Little and I couldn't be happier about it.

"What kind of surprise?" She asked, suckling on her pacifier. I wished that she was sucking on my cock instead, but as usual, I didn't say anything about that. I shouldn't.

"You are going to see," I purred before picking her up and taking her to the bathroom. "But first, I think that you need to brush your teeth."

"I don't want to brush my teeth. I don't like that," she complained, her voice sounding slightly altered thanks to the pacifier between her lips. It should be annoying me slightly, but it actually had the opposite effect.

"You *are* going to brush your teeth. Otherwise, I'm going to have to punish you."

Her eyes went wide in an instant.

"But what kind of punishment would that be? Are you going to... spank me?"

Spank her? I couldn't deny that the thought excited me, but that wasn't going to happen. Not so suddenly, anyway. Not to mention that I wasn't going to give Myrna exactly what she

wanted in such a short amount of time.
I just couldn't spoil her.

CHAPTER 10

Harold

I opened the bathroom door. I'd taken so many showers here and spent so much time that it was familiar to me. I loved the way that Myrna felt more comfortable after the death threats. They weren't showing up anymore, which meant that she felt safer with me.

"I really don't want to brush my teeth."

"You are going to have to brush your teeth one way or another. I'm your Daddy, remember? You have to do everything I want."

"It's not fair."

"It is and you know it."

She pursed her lips, but her pout wasn't going to stop me. I put her down on the floor and then she took out her pacifier. Good. I'd worried that she was going to be a little more reluctant about going on with this.

I grabbed the toothbrush, spread the toothpaste on the head, and then positioned myself behind her.

She looked at the toothbrush. It was one of the many she had. The brand was Hello Kitty and the head's bristles were soft and gentle. I was going to be gentle when brushing her teeth for the first time, so there was no chance that I was going to hurt her gum.

Not to mention that this wasn't the first time I was brushing someone's teeth. I had experience.

"I really don't like that I have to brush my teeth after eating the best breakfast in the world."

"Well, I can't risk you having dental problems in the future. Toothache is really bad and I would be irresponsible if I didn't do anything to prevent it."

She sighed.

"I suppose you're right. Still, I don't like it."

"You don't have to like anything. You just have to keep doing everything you want. Otherwise, you would lose access to the late-night cartoons that you like to binge watch."

"Oh, you really wouldn't do that."

"I would do that and so much more. Remember that I'm your Daddy and, from now on, I have full control over you."

She opened her mouth as if she was going to protest about that, but then she thought better about it. I slapped her butt slightly. This morning, she wore only a tiny, stretchy pair of panties, other than her knee-long shirt and her bra. Myrna could be wondering right now when I would finally diaper her for the first time.

"Fine, fine," she said under her breath and then opened her mouth. I put the head of the toothbrush between her lips and then I started to rub it left and right and up and down on her teeth.

The smell was that of mint, as was the taste. She liked it even though she would never admit something like that to me.

Some minutes later, I said, "fill your mouth with water and spit out the foam. We are almost done."

"Yes, Daddy," she grumbled. She didn't like brushing her teeth, but this was one of the reasons why I should be her caretaker. Myrna needed a guiding hand.

She was slow doing it as though she wanted to show me how much she hated brushing her teeth, but she eventually finished it. A couple of moments later, I repeated, "do the same again. I want to make sure that there's no more foam and toothpaste in your mouth."

"Yes, Daddy," she grumbled again before filling her mouth with water and then she spat it out. After that was over, I settled my hands on her shoulders after putting the toothbrush back on top of the sink.

"Open your mouth, Bitty. I want to make sure that there really is no more toothpaste in your mouth."

She connected her eyes with mine through the reflection in the mirror, squinting them slightly.

When she realized that I wasn't going to change my mind about this - after all, I was always strict and unwavering when it came to my decisions - she opened her mouth one more time.

I turned Myrna around slowly, checking the interior of her mouth with care and attention.

"One more time, Bitty."

"One more time?" She asked, her tone showing how incredulous she was right now.

She groaned before filling her mouth with water again. Bitty sloshed it back and forth between her cheeks and then spat it out into the sink.

After that was over, she turned around again and opened her mouth one more time. This time, I noticed that she opened her mouth wider as if she wanted to show me she gave her all and wasn't half-assing this part.

I lowered my head one more time and I put my hand under her chin. My eyes examined the interior of her mouth with the utmost attention and after determining that I was satisfied, I said, "good enough for me. I don't have to punish you anymore, Bitty."

"Finally," she grumbled again. "Pick me up, please?"

I wiped her mouth to make sure that there was no more foam left on it.

"Not this time. Put your pacifier back in your mouth. I don't want you to talk so much right now."

Before doing that, Myrna said, "and what else do you want to do with me?"

"Well, since you've been such a good girl and you've obeyed everything I wanted you to do when brushing your teeth, then I'm going to give you a treat. It's going to be big and it's going to take that thing you've been wanting to lose for so long."

Her eyes danced when I mentioned that. Bitty wasn't thinking, this morning, that I was going to take her virginity, but I could. My dick was rock hard and pre-come was already oozing out, thinking about it.

"If that's what you want me to do, then I'm already popping the pacifier back into my mouth."

And she did that and I took her hand before leading her to her bedroom. After doing that, I closed the door before pushing her until she was lying on her back on the mattress.

Myrna felt so small. I was going to be careful when taking her virginity. Still, I didn't have to worry much about that.

She could take everything I had.

CHAPTER 11

Myrna

Harold was on top of me. He moved his legs to both sides of my body and then he snuck his hands up my legs. I felt his fingers moving slowly over my body. His skin touched against my skin and made me feel goosebumps all over.

His fingers touched my labia with precision. The way that he pressed his fingers on my sensitive part sent electrical shocks in my body. My breathing stopped for a moment when he moved his body forward as he hid the light bulb hanging from the ceiling.

My eyes went up and down as I scrutinized every part of his body. Harold wasted no time before sneaking his finger inside my tunnel. He moved it forward and backward, and left and right. His movements were slow but precise. Everything was happening in slow motion, and I itched for the opportunity to kiss him again.

He neared his hand to my mouth and then he plucked out the pacifier. He chucked it over his shoulder and then he placed his hands on my cheeks. I wondered what was going on, and I had just about a couple seconds to wonder about that before he connected his lips to mine.

His lips were passionate and wet from the get-go. He pressed them all the way until I felt as though I couldn't breathe anymore. Moving my hands over his back, my fingers basked in the warmth coming from his body and the heat radiating from it.

Sweat drops trickled down his skin. Everything was so silent in my bedroom that I could even hear his heavy breathing. Feeling that just worshiping his body with my hands wasn't enough, I decided to go for something else. Before Harold could say anything about it, I snuck my fingers under his pants. Then, he lowered them for me and gave me access to what I was seeking.

His balls and gargantuan cock.

I wrapped my fingers around his shaft before I began to stroke it. My strokes were gentle and decisive during the moment this was happening. Pre-come began to ooze out of the tip, coating my fingers. Little giggles of pleasure escaped my mouth an instant later. Wanting now more than ever before to keep him locked up with me, I threw my legs around his body before thrusting it against mine.

He chuckled before saying, "for an infraction like that one, I think you need to be punished."

"You can punish me however you want, Daddy," I said before rubbing my legs on his lower backside. His muscles flexed and pressed back against my calves. It was as though his body had zero fat.

In the meantime, I continued to move my hand up and down along his shaft. It was over 8 inches long, without a shred of doubt. The smell of pre-come continued to permeate the air around my nose, and I could only keep on sniffing it so that I could continue to bask in the pleasure that came with it.

"You are so incredibly hungry, Little One. I bet that you are pretty tight as well, especially considering you are a virgin."

I groaned and threw my head back into the pillow when he lowered his body, ceiling light shining on my tired face. My cunt was already incredibly wet as my mind continued to obsess over how I was going to feel when he was splitting it open with his manhood.

"And I like your taste as well," he murmured while his head was still stuck between my legs. Then, he moved his hands and clamped his fingers on my thighs before he placed them over his shoulders.

After that was done, he lined up his cock to my waiting pussy. It vibrated in front of it. Smiling, Harold wasted no time before he started to press the tip of the gland inside. As he eased it in, I grabbed the pillow with my fingers, which dug into it strongly while he penetrated me all the way.

Pain flared up in me when he pierced my hymen. He was confident as he did that. Then, he went all the way inside of me as he bottomed me out. Little cries of pleasure escaped my mouth in succession until he started to piston in and out of me.

My pussy closed around his manhood strongly. I wasn't going to let go of it no matter what happened. His hips shot back and forth as he began to pound in and out of me, and a smile spread over my face as I started to match him thrust for thrust.

My rising orgasm burst inside of me and my body shook and trembled with intense pleasure. Harold didn't put on a condom, just like he had promised that he wouldn't when we fucked. My body melted when he creamed inside of me no more than a couple of minutes later. Panting, I noticed how much he lasted. He had so much energy in him!

Tightening my legs around his lower back, I told him that I didn't want him to move anywhere right now. After his eyes locked with me and he smiled one more time, he told me that he understood my wishes at the moment.

Before long, Harold finally pulled out, and then he collapsed on the bed with a huge, dazzling smile on his face. After we noticed that we were both panting, he pulled me a little closer to him and spooned me, pressing his cock onto my sore buttcheeks. It was his way to show me that I was his now more than ever before.

Who would have thought that me hiring a bodyguard to work for me was going to lead me to finding my Daddy?

The possibility just never crossed my mind.

HAROLD'S EPILOGUE

I was standing in front of my house and my girlfriend was coming out of her car. Even from afar, I could already smell the perfume of another man coming from her, and I wasn't imagining things.

It was really happening.

She wore expensive clothes which were probably given to her by her new man. I wondered who he was, but soon convinced myself that it didn't matter anyway. It just didn't.

Her blazer was fiery red. Her dark sunglasses stood out and her hair flew with grace in the wind. Her high-heeled boots clacked in front of the garage.

"Tell me that you were not really with someone else."

She sighed.

"I actually came here for my stuff. I really tried to make us work, but I think that I was just wasting my time."

"I was thinking the same thing."

There was a moment of silence between us.

"Are you going to tell me more about that?"

"Should I?" I taunted, shrugging. I didn't feel like explaining myself to Michelle no matter how much she acted as though she was hurt by the news.

She took a deep breath. "I suppose that there's no helping it. After you caught me…"

"You were cheating on me. I don't think there's anything you can say about that which can remediate our problems"

"I loved you."

A tear almost escaped. "I loved you too, but that's all in the past and there's nothing about it that we can do."

Another moment of silence hung in the air between us. It was mean and unforgiving. It was something we could never erase.

"Well, I came here to get my stuff and that's exactly what I'm going to do no matter how much you want to change this."

"I never said I want to change anything."

She shook her head before bursting past me as though she was a hurricane. Myrna was in her apartment and packing her stuff in her bags. Now that we had already discussed how to move forward after that incredible night when I took her virginity, we determined she was going to come to live with me. She was busy with that, so she wasn't going to see the mess that I was like right now.

I closed my eyes and took out my cigarette pack before getting one out. I lit it up with my lighter moments before Michelle burst out through the front door.

She rushed over to her car without turning her head to look at me and say goodbye. I didn't expect any different, coming from her. In fact, relief washed over me when she drove away and then took the next road before disappearing.

Birds chirped and sang in the trees as though the environment around me told me everything was going to be so much better from now on.

And I certainly hoped so. After all, Myrna was already coming here in the pickup truck I rented for her move-in day.

MYRNA'S EPILOGUE

So, that was it. We got married. We were happier now than ever before in our lives. I even told my parents about us and we shared a great night together. As for the death threats, they were a non-issue now. All the culprits were caught. In the end, it turned out that they weren't actually from the local church.

They were just overzealous fans who took it among themselves to expel me out of my apartment so that they could see me in person.

It didn't work out for them, though.

I'd thought that living in an apartment would provide me with the safety that I sought, but what was truly missing in my life was a partner. He was more than a boyfriend. Harold looked after me and always showed me how important I was to him.

It couldn't be any different, so I kissed him one more time. His lips were so tender. Just couldn't imagine myself spending any time anywhere else right now.

"Where are we going now, Daddy?" I asked, sitting by his side and letting his arm drop over my shoulders. He was driving. He was taking me somewhere.

He promised me that I was going to love it, and I sure as hell couldn't stop obsessing over it. No wonder the big bright smile on my face couldn't be erased.

"Don't worry, Little One. You are going to find out in a bit," he replied before kissing me one more time, and this time it was on my cheek. He took me to the other part of the town, where I jumped out of the pickup truck. I was wearing a Cinderella shirt and pink, childish boots. After realizing that Harold was always going to be on my side, I felt much safer being the person I was, even outside. It was so different from being the Little I was in my videos.

He took my hand and we bounced into the shop. My eyes scanned the interior for anything that stood out, and I soon found out the only thing that could be here waiting for me.

A big crib. It was big enough even for someone my size.

"Whoa. It's really so pretty," I said, rushing over to it and positioning myself all over it. Whether it was supposed to be mine or not, I was going to cherish it for as long as I could until we had to walk out of the shop.

"It's yours. It's ours. I bought it for you, Bitty," he murmured while placing his hands on my shoulders and nearing his head to my ear. Harold then kissed me one more time and this time it was on the nape of my neck.

I writhed and threw my arms over his shoulders, sealing my lips with his.

"I'm so happy, Daddy. I'm so happy that we are together and I love you so much."

"I love you too, Little One."

The End

Leave your review. Your feedback helps me improve a lot.

TEASER: DOCTOR'S PLUS SIZE LITTLE

Duty Calls - 4

"Are you going to tell me what you think is wrong with you?" The doctor asked. He was a man in his mid-30s, well built, and excitably handsome. I know, I know. That wasn't what I should be thinking about him, but what else was I going to be thinking about right now, especially when I was single and there was a secret about me that he could never find out about?

I mean, why the hell did I keep coming to our therapy sessions when I couldn't even tell him something so basic about me?

"Should I?" I asked, chuckling. This wasn't the first time we were meeting. In fact, it was the opposite of that. I lost count of how many sessions I already had with him.

And yet, he was still struggling to find out exactly what was wrong with me. I still thought it was just social anxiety that was ruining my life like this, but c'mon, that couldn't be the whole truth.

Either way, what was happening right now was that I was here in his therapy room, looking at the ceiling. He was seated by my side and his hand was holding his phone, which he was using to take notes about my answers.

Therapy with him was always weird, but there was a reason

why I always came here. Or maybe I should be saying that there were so many more reasons why I kept coming to his office.

"Look, we are going to keep making no progress as long as you keep withholding information from me," he explained, his tone showing that he wasn't here to play with me.

At least the therapy sessions were free. The government was paying for them. Finally, after paying taxes for so long in my life, the government was helping me with something.

"But, doc, it really is so difficult for me to talk about what's hurting me," I tried to explain, watching the ceiling fan spinning. It was spinning slowly. It didn't have to be turned on, though. The windows were open and cool air was coming from the outside.

To be honest, if I said that I was a Little, the first thing he would do would be to kick me out of the office without even attempting to hear the first thing about why I was like this.

He shook his head, sounding and looking disappointed. In the meantime, the only thing I could do was to check out and scrutinize the way that his hair slightly swayed, making me want to thread my fingers through them.

Actually, I wanted to do so much more with his body. It was such a pity that I never would be able to. Even though I couldn't see any signs that he was taken, there was no denying that he wasn't someone in my league, which meant that there was no reason to think he would ever look at me the same way.

I wanted to see how Paul looked without his uniform on. I was pretty sure that it wasn't common for doctors to look that hot, the muscles bulging and flexing under his uniform even though he wasn't doing much other than holding his phone in his hand as he continued to take notes about me.

Or was he doing something else? Maybe he was chatting with someone? Nah, that couldn't be it. He was a professional, I was certain.

His office and the therapy room were so clean. They were some of the reasons why I kept on coming back here. Back at home, my house wasn't so clean – at least, not as immaculate as this place was, that was.

"You're really making this so much more difficult than it should be."

"It's not my fault, really. I'm really trying to tell you everything about me, but every time I think about it, my mind goes blank."

"I still feel like you are withholding information from me on purpose. It feels like, to me, that you don't fully trust me. How many times do I have to tell you that I value patient privacy?"

I wished we had so much more than just privacy, but I wasn't going to complain. This was like my dirty secret, which was even more peculiar than me being a Little.

There. I thought that. I thought about my Little side, my littleness, pretending that I was like Anastasia. I liked her so much. She was so much like me and every time that I was in my apartment and completely alone, I dressed up like her.

But thinking about what my next words should be, there was no way that I was going to tell Paul anything about that. As I said, he would kick me out and tell sheriff Victor about me, and that was certainly not something I was willing to risk.

"I'm not withholding anything, I swear," I exclaimed, sitting up on the bed-couch combination piece of furniture where I was lying before. Just when I was going to say something else, I noticed that it was already time for me to leave his office, which was something that pained my heart - a lot more than it ever should.

"Your time is up, Desiree," Paul announced, standing up and slipping his phone back into his pocket.

I sighed, standing up.

"I'm really so sorry about being like this," I confessed, wishing things were different. I could already feel my depression sneaking in and I couldn't do anything about it. I couldn't do anything about it because of my loneliness.

And upon getting there, to my apartment, the first thing that would happen was to think about my loneliness. Really, I just couldn't seem to put that aside no matter how much I tried.

"You don't need to be sorry about it. Next time, when you come here, I'm sure that you will be able to tell me exactly what it is that is bothering you. Either that or I'm going to figure it out by myself."

But if that did happen, the worst would come to pass.

SIMILAR BOOKS

SERIES - MAFIA CUPIDS

A mafia setting with generous amounts of plus size dynamics.

1. His Plus Size Little
2. Hitman's Plus Size Little
3. Biker's Plus Size Little

SERIES - BIG ME

MM ABDL. Lots of age play, sweetness, peppered with steamy scenes, and sprinkled with age gap dynamics.

1. Pampering Little Miguel
2. Endless Crayons
3. Teaching Little Jerry

Or download all of these books in this bundle:

Sweet Holidays

ABOUT THE AUTHOR

Amanda King writes sweet ABDL, age play romances. Packaged with steamy scenes, her books are fast-paced and sprinkled with age gap dynamics.

When she isn't writing, she's reading for inspiration. Her most popular series is 'Mafia Cupids.'

www.ingramcontent.com/pod-product-compliance
Lightning Source LLC
Chambersburg PA
CBHW060916130726

48001CB00006B/2264